Spot the Sight Words
I Can Read

Bela Davis

abdobooks.com

Published by Abdo Kids, a division of ABDO, P.O. Box 398166, Minneapolis, Minnesota 55439. Copyright © 2023 by Abdo Consulting Group, Inc. International copyrights reserved in all countries. No part of this book may be reproduced in any form without written permission from the publisher. Abdo Kids Junior™ is a trademark and logo of Abdo Kids.

Printed in the United States of America, North Mankato, Minnesota.

052022

092022

Photo Credits: Getty Images, Shutterstock

Production Contributors: Teddy Borth, Jennie Forsberg, Grace Hansen

Design Contributors: Candice Keimig, Pakou Moua

Library of Congress Control Number: 2021950558

Publisher's Cataloging-in-Publication Data

Names: Davis, Bela, author.

Title: Spot the sight words: I can read / by Bela Davis.

Other Title: I can read

Description: Minneapolis, Minnesota : Abdo Kids, 2023 | Series: Spot the sight words | Includes online resources and index.

Identifiers: ISBN 9781098261610 (lib. bdg.) | ISBN 9781098262457 (ebook) | ISBN 9781098262877 (Read-to-Me ebook)

Subjects: LCSH: Sight-vocabulary method of reading--Juvenile literature. | Word recognition--Juvenile literature. | English language--Vocabulary--Juvenile literature. | Readers (Primary)--Juvenile literature.

Classification: DDC 372.462--dc23

Table of Contents

Spot the Sight Words . . 4

Did You Spot
the Words? 22

Glossary 23

Index 24

Abdo Kids Code 24

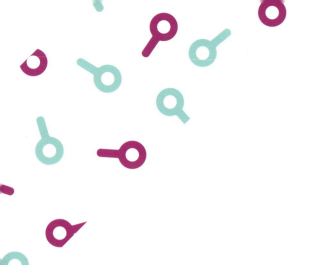

Spot the Sight Words

I can read.

I have one book.

I like this book.

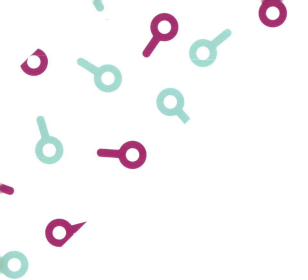

You can read.

You can read

You have one book.

You like your book.

your

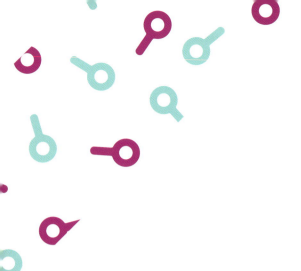

We can read.

We have two books.

I can read your book.

your

can read I book

15

You can read my book.

You can read book

We like to read.

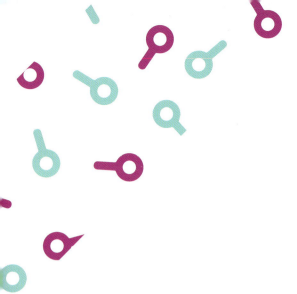

We like our books!

Did You Spot the Words?

Find the words!

Glossary

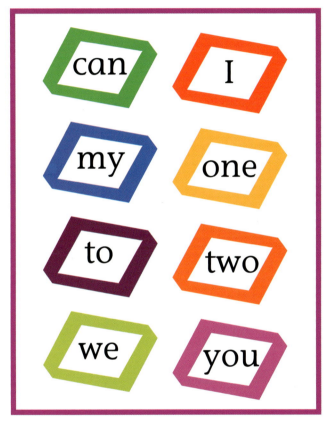

sight word
a common word that can be recognized instantly without having to sound out.

spot
to notice or catch sight of.

Index

can 4, 8, 12, 14, 16

have 6, 10, 12

I 4, 6, 14

like 6, 10, 18, 20

my 16

one 6, 10

our 20

this 6

to 18

two 12

we 12, 18, 20

you 8, 10, 16

your 10, 14

Visit **abdokids.com** to access crafts, games, videos, and more!

Use Abdo Kids code **SIK1610** or scan this QR code!